Yesternight...

A story for those whose days cannot contain all their dreams.

LINDA HOBGOOD

ISBN 978-1-64471-383-9 (Paperback)
ISBN 978-1-64471-384-6 (Hardcover)
ISBN 978-1-64471-385-3 (Digital)

Covenant Books, Inc.
11661 Hwy 707
Murrells Inlet, SC 29576
www.covenantbooks.com

For Claire with Love

Yesterday it rained. As tiny drops of spring showers splashed on the window panes, I wondered whether fairies' tiny feet make such sounds when they dance on budding flowers.

Then yesternight…

In the darkness of my room, the fairies came to dance! They invited me to join them, and as soon as I found my fairy gown and my wings, the fun began. We all held hands and twirled on tiptoe. Books on my bed became lily pads for us to leap across as we traversed the quilt lake. As Lovey bunny and Rudy reindeer watched from their pillow perch, the garden fairies flew from the bed to the dresser to the roof of the dollhouse and then to the roof of my house. Lovey and Rudy and I waved good-bye to the fairies, just as the sun was peeking through the trees.

Summer days are long and hot and filled with so much fun that no one wants to go inside. We played with bikes and balls and made chalk drawings on the driveway, and we tried hard not to hear Mommy and Daddy calling us inside for bath and bedtime. That was yesterday.

But yesternight…

Darkness crept into my bedroom, and suddenly Dog-dog and Dolly begged to go camping. Scrambling into my boots and jungle jacket, we piled pillows on top of each other and spread the quilt over the bedposts and the bookcase and the dollhouse and found ourselves in a tent on the banks of a giant river in a tropical rainforest! Stuffed snake slithered past our sleeping bags as overhead the tropical birds squawked and whistled in the trees on the banks of the rug that was our river. Dog-dog kept watch as Dolly and I slept, holding a compass, a flashlight, and a thermos full of fruit punch, which we shared. Suddenly, the river raged and the tent collapsed, and through the early dawn we scrambled to shore in my bed and woke up to another summer morning.

We could tell from the changing colors of the leaves that autumn was here. Mommy zipped us into our jackets before we ran to the swings and sliding board. I rode the glider and climbed the rock wall. The breeze blew my ponytail in the air, and I wondered all day yesterday what it might be like to ride a real pony.

So yesternight…

As Daddy finished bedtime story and turned out the light in the lamp on my dresser, I could hear the night horse tapping his hoof against the closet door. In the dark I donned my cowgirl boots and kerchief and my rawhide vest and skirt with fringe. Surprising him with a cube of sugar, I led the night horse out of the imaginary corral. He trotted beside the bed so I could climb on his back, and off we galloped! Down the stairs and out the door, around the corner, and off through the neighborhood, horsey galloped with the wind. His horsey tail and my ponytail flew behind us as we leaped over hillsides and fences, across fields and flower beds. We slowed to a steady gait at the driveway, and horsey let me dismount on the steps at my front door. I waved good-bye, scampered upstairs and into bed, just in time to hear Mommy call, "Good morning!"

Outside the frosty window by my bed were snow-covered housetops, benches, and hedges. Little sister had never seen anything like it! We were bundled in our snowsuits and mittens, hoping to build a snow family, sled downhill, lick icicles, and lie down to create snow angels, all before daytime turned to evening. Yesterday we bundled and lumbered, flopped and trudged in the snow.

Then yesternight…

Encore!

Magnifique

18

We danced! Snowflake ballerinas shone like stars everywhere in my bedroom. They told me they had come in search of a snow princess to lead their ballet. But she would have to have a tutu and tights, a tiara and toe shoes, and I told them they had come to the perfect place. In minutes we were floating, pirouetting, leaping, and lunging in graceful synchrony. Lovey bunny and Rudy reindeer, Stuffed snake, Dog-dog, Dolly, and porpoise clapped with breathless enthusiasm. They called "Encore" and "Magnifique," and we curtsied in appreciation. We twirled all night and just past dawn, leaving me almost no time to get back into my pajamas before my family opened my door to say, "Wake up time!" (They also asked why I was wearing a tiara).

All the fun we had yesterday led to coughing and sneezing and watery eyes. We were very concerned that this might mean having to stay indoors the next day. By suppertime even Mommy sounded sniffly. There was only one thing to do

and yesternight…

We planned a splendid tea party. The dolls love parties, and they offered to help. By moonlight we arranged a lovely table with a tablecloth and matching folded napkins. We set out our favorite cups and saucers. Using magic crayons and lined paper, we wrote invitations to the party and then decorated each one with hearts and flowers. We made delicious and pretty pretend cookies to accompany the warm tea. I put on my bonnet and coat over my apron and tiptoed down the hall to surprise Mommy with a cup of tea to make her feel better in the morning. Leaving a handmade get-well card on her bedside table that all the dolls had signed (so Mommy would know we were thinking of her), I tiptoed back to my room and woke to the sound of big brother asking who had been using all his crayons and what had happened to the paper from his first-grade writing tablet.

Yesterday we woke to find the snow had melted. Snow family's hats and scarves lay on the grass with no one to wear them. Sleds were propped against the wall inside the garage, their blades silent and dry. It was still cold, but we knew that soon tulips and daffodils would awaken from their winter sleep and bloom us into spring! Sun would shine, and we would be riding in a magic boat, skimming across the water, making waves in our wake, pausing to jump from the bow and splash into Daddy's waiting arms. Yes, indeed, yesterday was winter. But just wait

until yesternight…

When we will have sailed around the world before morning!

What else is nighttime for?
Sweet daydreams!

The End…
only the Beginning

About the Illustrator

Sarah Muse lives in Washington DC where she works as a graphic designer. When not working on her next project she is usually training for her next run or finding time to snuggle and play with the many dogs she has in her family.

About the Author

Photo credit: Robert Hodierne

Linda lives in Virginia, between the hills and the seashore, where she serves on the faculty of the University of Richmond. When she is not teaching rhetoric or coaching presentations with undergraduates, Linda and husband Jim delight in the lives of their three grandchildren.

CPSIA information can be obtained at www.ICGtesting.com
Printed in the USA
BVIW121046210819
556213BV00046B/144